# PRACTICING PATIENCE

## How to wait patiently when your body doesn't want to

**BOYS TOWN Press**

Boys Town, Nebraska

Written by
**JENNIFER LAW**

Illustrated by
**BRIAN MARTIN**

D1319509

**Practicing Patience**

Text and Illustrations Copyright © 2021 by Father Flanagan's Boys' Home
ISBN 978-1-944882-70-9

Published by the Boys Town Press, 13603 Flanagan Blvd., Boys Town, NE 68010

For a Boys Town Press catalog, call **1-800-282-6657**
or visit our website: **BoysTownPress.org**

Publisher's Cataloging-in-Publication Data

Names: Law, Jennifer, author. | Martin, Brian (Brian Michael), 1978- illustrator.

Title: Practicing patience : how to wait patiently when your body doesn't want to / written by Jennifer Law ; illustrated by Brian Martin.

Description: Boys Town, NE : Boys Town Press, [2021] | Audience: grades PreK-5, ages 4-11. | Summary: Gabe hates waiting, especially in the oh-so-slow lunch line. Lucky for him, his shoes know everything there is to know about being patient, even when it's hard, and share their wisdom with him.--Publisher.

Identifiers: ISBN: 978-1-944882-70-9

Subjects: LCSH: Patience--Juvenile fiction. | Shoes--Juvenile fiction. | Waiting (Philosophy)--Juvenile fiction. | Calmness--Juvenile fiction. | Emotions in children--Juvenile fiction. | Children--Life skills guides. | CYAC: Patience--Fiction. | Shoes--Fiction. | Waiting (Philosophy)--Fiction. | Calmness--Fiction. | Emotions--Fiction. | Behavior--Fiction. | Conduct of life. | BISAC: JUVENILE FICTION / Social Themes / Manners & Etiquette. | JUVENILE FICTION / Social Themes / Emotions & Feelings. | JUVENILE FICTION / Social Themes / Values & Virtues. | SELF-HELP / Self-Management / General. | EDUCATION / Counseling / General.

Classification: LCC: PZ7.1.L3829 P73 2021 | DDC: [Fic]--dc23

*Printed in the United States*
10 9 8 7 6 5 4 3 2 1

To access FREE downloadable coloring pages

**ACCESS:**
https://www.boystownpress.org/book-downloads

**ENTER:**
Your first and last names
Email address
Code: 944882pp709
Check yes to receive emails to ensure your email link is received

Saving Children    Healing Families

Boys Town Press is the publishing division of Boys Town, a national organization serving children and families.

HI!
MY NAME
IS GABE!

This is my story
about how I learned the

**MAGIC OF PATIENCE.**

**PATIENCE IS HARD. NO ONE LIKES TO WAIT.** Before, when I had to wait, my head would tell me to wait quietly, but my body didn't cooperate. It was like a burst of energy went from my toes to my nose!

4

A few days ago, I was at school. My teacher was calling people to line up for lunch.

SCHOOL

I was waiting for her to say my name. Well… kind of.

**It's SO hard to wait!**
*I was starving and people weren't getting quiet.*

5

I was talking to Elliott about playing soccer at recess. Next thing I knew, Mrs. Spencer sent everyone back to their desks to try it again. *It was taking forever!* I started bouncing my feet and tapping my pencil.

Then, a weird thing happened. I heard a voice coming from the floor. I looked down. My left shoe was talking! It said, **"Hi Gabe! I notice you're moving around a lot. It's hard to wait, isn't it?"** It was true, so I nodded.

It said, **"My name's Lefty.**
**I'm here to help you get on track.**
**When it's time to wait, try to:**

**Relax your body.**

**Pay attention.**

**Stay calm.**

**"Think of it as a moment to rest.** You don't have to go anywhere or do anything. In a way, it's a chance to save your energy for later — for something like recess or paying attention in class."

A talking shoe was definitely weird,
but this one made some sense.

I set my pencil down. I rested my hands on my desk and sat there. Boy! It was boring at first! I kept resting, and then I noticed it actually felt kind of peaceful.

I didn't have to go anywhere or do anything—just like Lefty said.
Pretty soon it was my turn to line up.

Later that day, I was in line to get a drink of water. *Everyone was taking so long!* Didn't they care that the rest of us wanted water, too? Then, I heard a different voice coming from the floor.

I looked down at my right shoe. It said,

**"Hey, Gabe! Could you use another idea about how to be patient?"**

13

I was surprised again, but I was ready to listen.

**"My name is Lacey."**

"Lacey?" I said. "As in laces in your shoes?"

**"Yep, just like shoelaces."**

"Your name's not Righty?" I asked.

"Of course not." Then, Lacey said, **"Another way to practice patience is to think positively. Are you thinking negatively about your situation right now?"**

### Hmm... that's funny... I was!

Lacey said, "Instead, try thinking, 'I can do this. I'm just waiting for my turn. The line won't last forever. It's already moving.'"

Since I was there and didn't have anything to do, I tried out the positive thinking. "I've been in lines before. We're all thirsty. I'm just waiting for my turn. I can handle this." *I did feel better!*

The next day, I was playing soccer at recess. My team was doing great! We were ahead by one when recess ended. The other team asked if we could keep playing at the next recess. We all agreed we would. I could hardly wait!

But, that's exactly what I had to do. Wait and wait . . . and wait.

# BORING!
## WHY COULDN'T MATH JUST BE OVER?

I stopped listening to Mrs. Spencer.

Then, I heard Lefty say, **"I notice you're having trouble waiting again. You're excited about the game, aren't you?"**

"Yes!" I said.

Lacey said, **"It's great to be excited but when you're only thinking about the game, it feels like time moves slowly. If you distract yourself, time seems to go faster. Getting busy with something else is a great way to practice patience."**

**"Right now the best thing to focus on is math,"** said Lefty. "Sometimes it could be something else, like what you'll do after school, a book you're reading, or a game you like to play. But since you'll be responsible for what Mrs. Spencer is saying anyway, math is the perfect thing to take your mind off the soccer game."

"Okay," I said, "I'll focus on math." And that's what I did. I listened to Mrs. Spencer and did the math worksheet. Then, it was time for recess! *It worked!*

The next day, Mrs. Spencer was waiting for our line to get quiet before we could go to P.E. I started walking away from the line and then back into it. I talked to Kendra, who was behind me, and then I walked away again.

Lacey said, **"Hey – what are you doing? The line is over there. When you wait in a line, you need to stay in the line.** You can't leave it and come back. You might lose your spot and you aren't following your teacher's directions when you do that."

"It's too hard," I said. "I can't just stand there and do nothing."

**"Yes you can,"** said Lefty.

"That's exactly what you are supposed to do. You are in a line to hold your spot until it's your turn for something. Think of you and your classmates as one set of shoes. If everyone started going separate ways and doing different things, your class wouldn't be able to function very well."

"Your teacher wouldn't be able to teach all of you at the same time. And things like getting a drink or traveling in the hallway wouldn't go as smoothly. **You all need to work together to make your whole class successful.**"

Lacey added, **"Right! It's like Lefty and me!**
If he went one way and I went another way, you wouldn't actually be able to go anywhere. We need to take turns to move together. It's the same for you and your classmates. Lines are a good way to move together. They give everyone a turn and help people safely travel to where they need to go."

I knew Lefty and Lacey were right.
I've even seen my parents in lines,
like at the store or when they drive.
I turned back and joined the line.

I stood there…waiting. I let my body rest and while I waited, I knew I was being helpful so that my class could travel to P.E.

Finally, my class was ready. I noticed I was ready, too! I looked down at my shoes. Lefty said, **"You've got it now!"** Lacey said, **"Keep it up!"**

# THANKS TO MY SHOES I'VE LEARNED A LOT ABOUT PATIENCE.

Patience is hard, but it's important. And I am still working on it because I want to be helpful and work with the people around me.

*To practice patience I can let my body rest and recharge, get busy with something else, or think positively.*

When I do these things, it makes it easier for me and the people around me.

## BEING PATIENT FEELS GOOD!

# TIPS FOR PARENTS AND EDUCATORS

**There's a saying we've all heard, that patience is a virtue. It's also a really important life skill – and one that is tough for most young people and many adults.** Helping children learn how to practice patience by staying calm and waiting their turn will set them up for success later in life. The tips below will help!

**1. Stand by your words.** If you tell a child he or she needs to wait, keep your word. For example, if a child has been told to wait and she keeps asking questions or crying, and you let her stop waiting and do what she wants, you are teaching her that this inappropriate behavior works. She will most likely behave that same way the next time she doesn't want to wait.

**2. Be calm.** It may be difficult, but when you look and act calm while waiting, it makes it easier for others around you to be calm and patient as well.

**3. Play.** Teach children they can have fun even while waiting. You can start an "I Spy" game or have them guess a number between 1 and 100.

**4. Create a mental distraction.** Start singing a song while you wait. "Old McDonald" works great with younger children. Seasonal songs can work well, too, like "Jingle Bells."

**5. Stay physically busy.** Help children do something to get their minds off what they are waiting for. Help them be busy. They could read a book, watch a movie, draw a picture, play with toys, play a board game, and more.

**6. Standing in line doesn't have to look like just standing in line.** You could use this time to incorporate some mindfulness with deep breaths and a few yoga poses. Mountain Pose and Eagle Pose could be great to try here. Not only can it add fun to waiting, but balancing can enhance focus, too. It's a win-win.

**7. Model being patient.** When you are in line at the store or in traffic, be okay with that. Model the strategies described in the book. Children are watching and learning from you.

**8. Talk about it.** When you are waiting for something, you can talk about what you look forward to or what you are worried about. Start conversations with children about what they are looking forward to or what might be worrying them. Be ready to listen.

**9. Celebrate when the wait is over!** Enjoy whatever it is you were waiting for! Remind them it was worth the wait.

For more parenting information, visit boystown.org/parenting.

BOYS TOWN®
Saving Children   Healing Families

# Boys Town Press books
## *Kid-friendly books for teaching social skills*

A book series by Jennifer Law for grades PreK-5 that teaches difficult but important skills, like staying calm, practicing patience, and getting along with others.

978-1-944882-49-5

978-1-944882-70-9

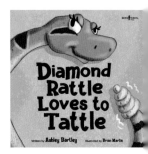

978-1-944882-57-0

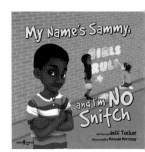

978-1-944882-61-7

A book series to help kids master social situations.

**Downloadable Activities**
*Go to BoysTownPress.org to download.*

978-1-944882-52-5

*OTHER TITLES: Parker Plum and the Rotten Egg Thoughts, Parker Plum & the Journey Through the CATacombs*

978-1-9-44882-34-1

978-1-9-44882-42-6

978-1-944882-54-9

*OTHER TITLES:*
*Freddie the Fly: Motormouth,*
*Freddie the Fly: Connecting the Dots*

**BOYS TOWN** ®
Press

**For information on Boys Town and its Education Model, Common Sense Parenting®, and training programs:**
boystowntraining.org | boystown.org/parenting
training@BoysTown.org | 1-800-545-5771

**For parenting and educational books and other resources:**
BoysTownPress.org
btpress@BoysTown.org | 1-800-282-6657